# RALPH WRECKS THIS BOOK!

## Illustrated by the **Disney Storybook Art Team**

A Random House PICTUREBACK® Book

Random House  New York

Copyright © 2018 Disney Enterprises, Inc. All right reserved. Published in the United States by Random House Children's Books, a division of Penguin Random House LLC, 1745 Broadway, New York, NY 10019, and in Canada by Penguin Random House Canada Limited, Toronto. Pictureback, Random House, and the Random House colophon are trademarks of Penguin Random House LLC. Golden Books, A Golden Book, A Little Golden Book, the G colophon, and the distinctive gold spine are registered trademarks of Penguin Random House LLC.
rhcbooks.com
ISBN 978-0-7364-3769-1
Printed in the United States of America
10 9 8 7 6 5 4 3 2 1

# Prologue

## Welcome to Litwak's Family Fun Center

For more than thirty years, Litwak's Family Fun Center had been entertaining children. Two generations of kids knew that if you wanted to play the best video games, Litwak's was *the* place to go.

The atmosphere in the arcade was one of ringing bells

But Felix wasn't the most ex͟͟͟͟ game.
That honor ͟͟͟͟ Guy Wreck-It Ralph.

Wheneve͟͟͟ kid ͟͟͟ ͟͟͟ ͟͟͟ple,
Ralph leaped on-sc͟͟͟ ͟͟͟ ͟͟͟ d
a furious attitude, ͟͟͟ ͟͟͟ w͟͟͟

As each game st͟͟͟ ͟͟͟ p͟͟͟
pixilated apartme͟͟͟ ͟͟͟ e ca͟͟͟
and smashed the͟͟͟ ͟͟͟ pieces. Bricks rained
down while fright͟͟͟ ders peered out from the
windows.

"FIX IT, FELIX ͟͟͟ nders wou͟͟͟
͟͟͟ heerful an͟͟͟
his m͟͟͟
skillfully
of the apartment ͟͟͟ windows
and loose bricks.

Once Felix fixed the entire building and reached the

> Wait . . . what? I'm NOT supposed to wreck this book? But that's what I do! Okay, okay, I got it. No more messing up the pages.

magic hammer

5

gets a medal.

The winne
all

What's up, friendo?

Hey, V. You need to see this book! It's all about us!

This is my favorite part—when we build your race kart in King Candy's garage.

Ahhh, the memories.

I know I shouldn't be wrecking this book, but it's so much fuuuuuuun!

**Aaahhh!** Okay, that was not a good idea. Now I'm all wrapped up in words!

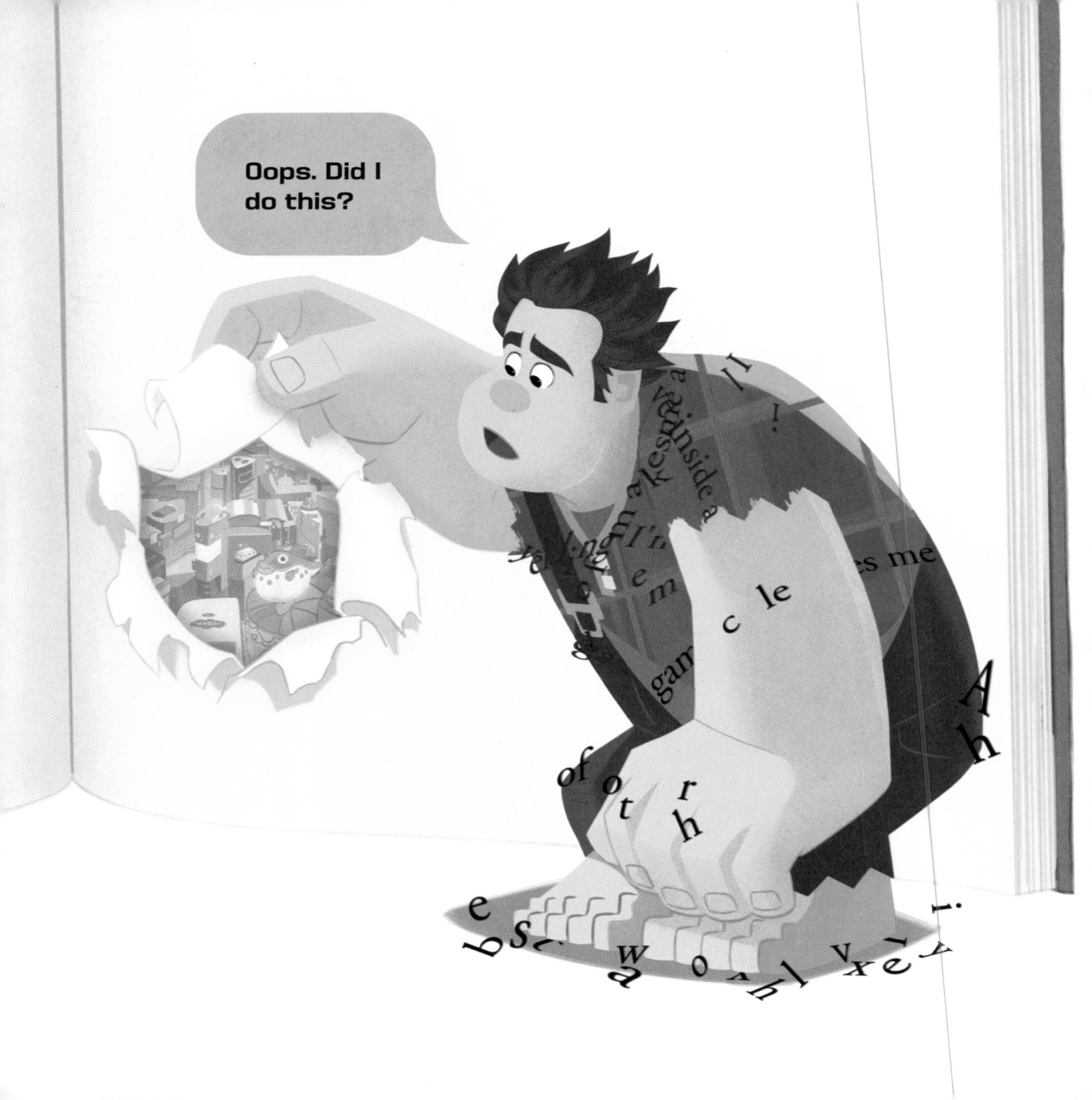
Oops. Did I do this?

There—that's better. They should call me Fix-It Ralph from now on.

But these words are making me itch. Maybe Vanellope can help me get them off.